At Grandma's

Rhonda Gowler Greene

illustrated by Karla Firehammer

Henry Holt and Company
New York

Henry Holt and Company, LLC, *Publishers since 1866*
115 West 18th Street, New York, New York 10011
www.henryholt.com

Henry Holt is a registered trademark of Henry Holt and Company, LLC
Text copyright © 2003 by Rhonda Gowler Greene
Illustrations copyright © 2003 by Karla Firehammer
All rights reserved.
Distributed in Canada by H. B. Fenn and Company Ltd.

Library of Congress Cataloging-in-Publication Data
Greene, Rhonda Gowler.
At grandma's / by Rhonda Gowler Greene; illustrated by Karla Firehammer.
Summary: Rhyming text describes the joys of an overnight visit to Grandma's house.
[1. Grandmothers—Fiction. 2. Sleepovers—Fiction. 3. Stories in rhyme.]
I. Firehammer, Karla, ill. II. Title.
PZ8.3.G824 At 2003   [E]—dc21   2002001757

ISBN 0-8050-6336-6 / First Edition—2003 / Designed by Amy Manzo
Printed in the United States of America on acid-free paper. ∞

10 9 8 7 6 5 4 3 2 1

The artist used acrylic on illustration board
to create the illustrations for this book.

*For my daughter, Lianna, and her best
buddies, Kippy and Poodle Puddles*
— R. G. G.

For Delaney and Riley
— K. F.

Big bed

Yellow sun

Breakfast bread with cinnamon

Overalls

Floppy hat

Bowl of cream for Grandma's cat

Squirrels to feed

Bluebirds too

A ride in Grandma's red canoe

Walking stick

Winding trail

Juicy berries and a pail

Lunch for two
Hungry guests
Noisy ducklings in a nest

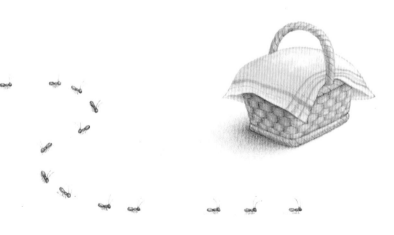

Raindrop splat

Summer shower

Ladybug and bright sunflower

Wooden bridge

White-cloud sky

Cattails and a butterfly

Mailbox full

Turtle shell

Buttercups to stop and smell

Garden patch

Rake and hoe

Carrots sprouting in a row

Fence to mend

Lemonade

Maple tree for resting shade

Pot and spoon

Golden light

Noodle soup that tastes just right

Starry sky

Fireflies

Night frogs singing lullabies

Cups of tea

Pie to eat

Bunny slippers on four feet

Favorite book

Flannel lap

Cat curled cozy in a nap

Big bed

Silver light

Hug and kiss . . . to say good night.